Altered Creatures Epic Fantasy Adventures
Prequel to the Thorik Dain Series

Treasure of Sorat

Read more free stories and
further Adventures of Thorik Dain at
www.AlteredCreatures.com

Copyright © 2015 by Anthony G. Wedgeworth
Published by Anthony G. Wedgeworth
Artwork by Frederick L. Wedgeworth

ISBN-13: 978-1508876632
ISBN-10: 1508876630

Altered Creatures Epic Fantasy Adventures
Thorik Dain Series
Book 0.8, Revision 1.2
Treasure of Sorat
www.AlteredCreatures.com

Without limiting the rights under the copyright reserved above, no part of this publication may be reproduced, stored in or introduced into retrieval system, or transmitted, in any form or by and means (electronic, mechanical, photocopying, recording, or otherwise), without the prior written permission of copyright owner of this book.

The scanning, uploading, and distribution of this book via the Internet or via any other means without the permission of the copyright owner is illegal and punishable by law. Please purchase only authorized electronic editions, and do not participate in or encourage electronic piracy of copyright materials.
Your support of the author's rights is appreciated.

This is a work of fiction. Names, characters, places, and incidents either are the product of the author's imagination or are used fictitiously, and any resemblance to actual persons, living or dead, business establishments, events, or locales is entirely coincidental.

No Thrashers or Chuttlebeast were harmed in the making of this book.

Altered Creatures Epic Fantasy Adventures
Prequel to the Thorik Dain Series

Treasure of Sorat

White Summit
Bay of Sorrows
MOUNTAINS
Kingsfoot
King's Valley
Farbank
Longfield
Rodent Buttes
FOREST
Pyrth
Shoreview
Waterrun
Bridgegate
Angry Sisters
Lake Fire
Victory
Portlock
West Dove
DOVEN
Veil
Luthralum Tunia
Lu'Tythis
Pelonthal City

Chapter 1
Alone with everyone

Thorik Dain sat at the wooden table and drew another small waterfall on the map he had been working on for months. Taxing his memory of his travels with his parents, he worked diligently to ensure the map was as accurate as possible while attempting to reveal the mysteries of what existed beyond their small village of Farbank.

Staring at his work, he visualized his experiences with his father when they explored the ancient path north to Kingsfoot. He then recalled his ventures on the far side of the great river near Spirit Peak, where his mother tracked game, his father hunted it, and he recorded the land and the creatures they found along the way.

It was hard to say why such a young boy was obsessed with recording and logging so much information about the outside world, but it was clear that he was so focused that he failed to notice the fun and merriment which surrounded him.

Several of the locals were playing music as the villagers danced and laughed under various large tents within the outdoor common area, which resided just downstream of Farbank. Children raced about without a care in the world as to what the future had in store for them. Elder villagers sat in groups telling tales of the past which had grown more dramatic since the last time the others had heard them. Food and drink were plentiful and excitement was in the air for the here and now. No one seemed to be concerned with events beyond today or past the boundaries of the village. Life was simple for those that lived there.

This was true for all except young Thorik Dain. Writing another note, he popped his head up when his mother ran from the dance area to pull him from his maps. "Mum, not now. I'm in the middle of logging our last trek."

"You can play with your papers later, son. But for now, you will be a part of this celebration and dance with me." Pulling him from the table, she nearly dragged him to the open area to dance with the rest of the adults. A quick curtsy to her partner was custom before they started, which he returned with a half-hearted bow. It was quickly followed by skipping about, locking arms, spinning each other, letting go, and twirling away before finding another partner to start the process over again.

Thorik continued for a few dances, but his eyes continued to revert back to the maps on the table. His concerns grew about them being knocked to the floor and stepped on. He finally excused himself and raced back to where he had been seated earlier.

"I thought your mum wanted you to dance." The voice of Thorik's father was always well balanced. Never too stern and never wimpy. One might say it was quite casual in manner.

"I did." His eyes never left the papers on the table, which he gathered together to prevent any from being lost.

"I know. But you missed the point. She wants you to be engaged in activities that interact with friends and family. She's concerned your life will consist of being alone."

"But I'm not alone. I'm here at the celebration, just as you asked."

"And yet, you're still here by yourself."

Thorik didn't make eye contact. After rolling up his maps, he tied some twine around them to ensure they stayed together. "I just wanted to make sure I had everything recorded from yesterday's trek before I forget anything."

Thorik's father sat next to him and watched the locals on the dance floor. "You know, son, I was much like you when I was your age. My head was so focused on things beyond my control that I was missing life. At least until I met your mum…and your grandmother, Gluic. They taught me how to enjoy the present-day and be involved in the experience of living. I wish I knew how to teach this to you." Taking a deep breath, he recalled his own younger years. However, he quickly realized that Thorik was more focused on the knots in the twine than on his father's comments. "Are you listening, Thorik?"

The youth nodded as he gathered another group of papers together. "I wish I had something to put all of these in."

Smiling at his son, he chuckled. "Yes, you are without a doubt my son."

Glancing up, he finally looked into his father's eyes. "Are we still heading past Fawn Hallow tomorrow for my birthday? I'm missing the southern ridge on my maps."

"One of these years I will give you a real gift, a unique present that shows you how special you are, instead of just another day of mapping the land."

"You say that every year, father," he said with a grin. "But I understand we can't afford any such luxuries. Besides, I enjoy traveling with you and mapping new valleys."

Though disappointed in himself for never coming through on a unique gift to his son, he was proud of how his son took the news. "I'll make you a deal. We'll head out for your survey mission if you have at least one more dance with your mum."

"Deal!" Thorik quickly agreed. Untying a twine from one of the scrolled up maps, he pointed to a location where he would like to travel.

Not budging from his stance, he raised an eyebrow as he waited. "Dance comes first. Than we can discuss our travel plans."
His deep sigh was overly played out before he handed his father his maps and headed to the dance floor, where his mum was ecstatic to see him.

Chapter 2
Su'l Sorat

The next morning, Thorik walked along the well-groomed path which led from the family's small home all the way downstream to the village. Spring's vibrant colors and smells filled the wooded hills on both sides of the mighty King's River Valley. It was a beautiful morning, and the youth was excited for the day of exploration. To prepare for it, he had collected all of his maps and was heading to the village to find a container with which to store them.

He had taken the trip to the village more times than he could count and had been surprised over the years by finding fallen trees, deer crossing his path, and once even a wild boar. However, today was unique. There, on the only path leading upstream from the village, was a traveler walking his way. Not just any outsider; this was a Human, a species which typically stood about a head taller than the Nums of the village. They also didn't grow soul-markings on their skin after they came of age. In addition, their hair tended be of one color or salted with grey. Thorik had never seen a Human before, but the stories and descriptions he had heard matched this man spot on.

"Hello, young Num. How are you on this fine day?"

Slightly nervous, Thorik hesitated. "I am fine."

"Just fine? It's a beautiful morning for an adventure."

"Adventure? Yes, it is. Especially seeing that it's my birthday."

"Well, congratulations on surviving another year, fine lad. I am Su'l Sorat. Who might you be?"

"I am Thorik Dain of Farbank." It was customary for Nums to always include the name of their residence, so Thorik found it odd that Humans did not. "I've never met anyone from outside the King's River Valley before. What is your business here?"

"Thorik Dain of Farbank, you say? It is a great pleasure to meet you." Reaching out to shake the Num's hand, he waited for Thorik to strategically wedge various maps under his other arm to free up a hand to shake. "What is it that you have tucked away which limits your movement?"

"What? Oh, these? They are drawings and notes of the area."

"Maps of the area? Wonderful. I'm new to the area and I'm somewhat lost. I've come here searching for something with no luck. Perhaps your maps may come in handy find my way. May I look at them?"

Hesitant to hand over his prized possessions, Thorik's eyes darted back and forth from his papers to Su'I. "I'm not comfortable setting them on the ground. They will get dirty or ripped.

Su'I nodded. "I understand. They are very important to you." After a moment of thinking, he reached into a large side-bag and dug around for a few moments before pulling out a wooden coffer. "This small box is normally used to store money, but I've used it to store important documents before. Why don't you see if your maps will fit within it?"

"Oh, I couldn't take it from you. It wouldn't feel right."

"Lad, you have a need for it, and I do not. Besides, you mentioned it was your birthday. Let this be my gift to you on this special day. It is unique. I doubt you'll run across another like it."

The wooden coffer appeared well crafted, and it had a sturdy latch on the front. It would surely keep Thorik's maps and notes away from harm and allow him to free up his arms. "Thank you, Mr. Sorat. That's very nice of you."

Opening the box, Su'I held the lid back while Thorik set the maps down one at a time in their new home. Once they were all in, Su'I closed the lid, latched the clasp, and then handed it to the youth. "There you go. That seems much better. So, now that you have a place for them, what do you say about allowing me to look at a few?"

"Of course. But I don't know the lands like my parents. You should talk to them. They know these valleys better than anyone."

"Then let us be on our way."

Following the path back upstream, they rounded a corner and headed toward a rocky hillside. Just prior to the vertical rocks sat a small, yet sturdy, one room cottage with a thin plume of smoke slowly rising from its chimney. Thorik's father was outside cutting wood for the fire, while his mother was busy inside the home preparing for their family venture upstream.

"Father! Come meet Su'I Sorat. He gave me this box for my birthday!"

Looking up from his wood pile, he was surprised to see a Human. "Greetings, friend. What brings you to these parts?" His voice carried loud enough to catch his wife's attention from inside the cottage.

Su'I followed Thorik and placed a light hand upon the youth's head before playfully making a mess of the various brown tones of hair. "Your son tells me that you know this area well."

"That is true. I have hunted these lands upstream of Farbank all my life. None know them better than my wife and I."

"That is excellent news, for I am in search of something which has been lost for far too long. Fortunately, I've been told what the valley looks like, along with a description of a few key rock landmarks. If I gave you this information, could you lead me to it?"

"These mountain ranges are filled with hundreds of little valleys, and each has countless rock formations and unique traits. The odds of you being able to provide enough information for us to know the exact location would be slim."

"Could it hurt to try?"

Taking a moment to consider the request, he noticed Thorik observing him. His answer to the man would teach his son a lesson on working with others, so his reply needed to reflect good parenting. "There is no harm in trying. Please come in and meet my lovely wife. We can chat over a cup of hot tea."

Nodding his appreciation, Su'I followed Thorik and his father into the cottage to meet his mother before discussing the location of the lost item. "The items are across the great river from Farbank."

Thorik's mother cleaned off the table before tending to the tea. "What items are those?"

"There are many great treasures in this world." Su'I pulled out a chair and sat at the table. "Many of which will never be found again. Some have powers. Others provide grand wealth."

"We have no need for either of those in Farbank, and I would be surprised if anything of such nature would find its way into the King's River Valley. The Mountain King was never one for these ideas, nor are his followers."

"True, but there are other types of treasures that are worth finding."

"Such as?"

"Having a piece of history. Knowing you are touching the very items that existed when great deeds were performed and handled by those heroes of the past."

"Artifacts? We have found ancient ruins in the hills, but there is nothing of value in them."

"Perhaps you're right. However, it's my understanding that these specific artifacts, as you said, are still there, waiting to be unearthed."

"What is it you're searching for?"

"It's actually several items. I'm in search of the original Runestones used by the Mountain King himself."

Laughing at the idea, Thorik's father fell into the seat at the table across from Su'I. "I have heard of such legends, but many attempts have been made without any fortune in finding them. What makes you believe they even exist?"

"The great and powerful Oracle, Deleth, informed me that they are here in this region. His powers of insight are greater than any other."

"Oracle?" Thorik glanced back and forth from each of his parents, waiting for an explanation.

His mother finally spoke up. "My brother, Brimmelle, has told me about Oracles. There are only a few left. They are the last remaining species of the civilization that the great Mountain King defeated in order to free us from slavery."

"That's correct," Su'I added. "Deleth has great powers, and he says the King's Runestones were not destroyed, as most have been taught."

"Why would he want them? And why would you search for them?"

Thorik could hear concern in his mother's voice, and searched his father's face for a reaction as well, only to find him calmly listening to the conversation without providing any visible emotions.

Raising a hand to slow her emotional response, Su'I gave a pleasant grin. "He does not want them. They are a symbol of his fallen people. I, on the other hand, am an explorer who wishes to find the truth in the Mountain King's War. For, along with the Runestones, there are records of these events that will shed light on what really happened. In a way, you could say that I am a truth explorer."

Thorik's parent's stayed quiet for a few moments, causing an uneasy tension which didn't break until his father spoke up. "If the King's Runestones truly exist, we would not want them to leave this valley. They should belong to the Nums."

Sighing at the statement, Su'I Sorat glared at the man across from him for a few seconds before speaking. "I understand your reluctance. They are unique and are part of your heritage, not mine." Pushing his chair out, he stood up tall and thanked them for their time. "I will be on my way to continue my search for the truth of our history. Good day."

After he left the cottage, the silence was fused with energy. Everyone wanted to talk first but no one did until seconds later when a flood of words collided over the surface of the table.

Once the verbal mess dissipated, Thorik's mother spoke again. "The King's Runestones? If they truly still exist, the Nums should keep them instead of the Humans or any of the other species beyond these mountains."

Thorik looked confused. "What's so special about these stones?"

His mother's eyes became glossy with excitement. "They are a symbol of our freedom, filled with the energy and emotions of all those who have held them before us. Touching them, we could feel the life force of the Mountain King himself. And without them, our culture would not have come to exist."

Clearing his throat, Thorik's father corrected her in the tone of a scholar pleasantly teaching a class. "What your mother means is that, without the Mountain King, our freedom and culture would not exist. The Runestones are just that, stones and gems. They have no value. They are simply objects that represent various teachings of the King. So in a way, he has reached out and touched us through these symbols."

Smiling at her husband's attempt to remove any illogical spiritual nature from her description, she played along. "Yes, and as you know from your academics in Kingsfoot, symbols are very important. Do you want them to be taken away?"

Nodding at his wife, his voice softened. "Of course not, but Su'I Sorat will not find them without us, and we most likely won't find them without him." Looking into his son's eyes, he could see the desire to explore and learn, just as he had in his youth. A slight chuckle began to fill his speech. "And they would have made such a unique birthday gift." He gave a wink to his son. "Perhaps someday."

Thorik could see the adventure slipping away from their grasp. He knew how much his mother and his grandmother, Gluic, enjoyed experiencing the magical feeling of the unknown. The thrill of discovery had hooked him as well. "What if we made a deal with him?"

"Deal?" Again, his father's voice was calm and studious. "What kind of transaction is forming in that head of yours, my little pioneer?"

"What if we told him we would help him if he allowed us to keep the Runestones, while he kept the records of the past?"

A devious smile crossed his mother's face as she turned to her husband with wide eyes, waiting for his answer. "That sounds fair to me."

Shaking his head back and forth, Thorik's father began to laugh. "Gluic has corrupted you both. You know that, don't you?" He eventually broke into a smile. "Fine. Go ask him. But you're going to have to answer to Fir Brimmelle about this when he finds out we helped an outsider."

Giving her husband a strong hug, she looked up with a childish grin. "Leave my brother to me. He'll get mad, but he always forgives me." Tilting her head, she continued with a laugh, "Then again, he's still mad that I married you."

"Thank you, father!" Thorik quickly turned and ran out of the house to find Su'I Sorat.

Chapter 3
Treasure's Location

That evening, after returning from Fawn Hallow, Thorik and his parents sat down to a meal with their new friend, Su'I Sorat. The dishes hadn't even been cleaned up before Thorik began pulling his maps from his new coffer and placing them across the table as he told Su'I of the adventure the outsider had missed earlier that day.

Filling his pipe with a bit of tobacco and leaning back in his chair, Thorik's father watched his son's excitement fill the room with his stories.

Map after map was unfolded and straightened out to fit up with other maps, showing large portions of the King's River Valley. "We've found bright red barked trees in this area and purple grass in the east side of this valley." Thorik went on and on about his ventures and the plants and animals he had seen.

His mother finally stopped him by placing a soft hand on his shoulder to get his attention. "Son, why don't you give Su'I a chance to tell us what he's looking for."

All focus was now on the outsider; Thorik and his mother stood at the table while his father continued to sit in his nice chair. The moment had finally come for everyone to learn what Su'I knew about the location.

Su'I leaned over the table and gazed at the maps. "I was informed that they are near Farbank." He pulled out a map of his own; it charted out a small section of a single valley with a cave system leading into the hillside. "Once we get in the correct valley, I believe this will lead us directly to it.

"That's not much to go on. There are many valleys with caverns in these mountains." Lighting his pipe, Thorik's father stayed back from the table in an effort to not get pulled into the excitement. A level head was needed.

"Agreed," Su'I acknowledged. "But I have more. The Oracle informed me that I must follow the path of Grazers into the old man's mouth, and then the tall ghost reveals upon three hands of light the way to travel."

A moment of silence was followed by Thorik laughing. "We have to find a ghost with three hands to point at a herd of Grazers inside an old man?" His sentence trailed off as he noticed his parents staring at each other with concern. "What's the matter?"

Walking up to the table, Thorik's father pulled the pipe from his mouth. "Do you think he's talking about Spirit Peak? Which one? There are three such rock towers."

She nodded. "It could be, but it will be difficult to determine which trail to follow. There are Grazer trails all over these mountain foothills. What do you think the old man's mouth would be? A grouping of wide-mouth orchids, a hillside cavity, or a perhaps a ring of Deadman Daisy flowers?"

"The phrase 'Hands of light' is an old expression for hours past sunrise or before sunset," Thorik's father added.

Su'I grinned. "I think if we travel to this Spirit Peak, it will lead us to the correct path, which will in turn lead us to the mouth and the valley beyond."

Thorik was filled with exhilaration over the entire discussion as he studied Su'I Sorat's map. "When do we leave?"

Taking a puff of his pipe, his father glanced down at him. "We do not."

"What? Why?"

"Spirit Peak is far too dangerous for someone your age. It is a trek for Nums who have fully come into their soul-markings. Therefore, if we go, you will need to stay behind and wait for us. I will not risk your life on such a hazardous hike."

Agreeing with him, Thorik's mother gave a slight nod. "You can stay with your Uncle Brimmelle at your grandmother's home." Seeing the protest in his eyes, she nipped the topic off before it became an argument. "Not this time, Thorik. When you get older you will have plenty of adventures outside of Farbank."

"But it's my birthday."

"Yes it is, and your father already told you that the Runestones are yours, if found." Walking from the table, she smiled at her own little gift. "I also have a present for you."

"I thought our trip to Fawn Hollow was my present from both of you."

"It was. But this one is just from me." Opening a wide wooden chest, she pulled back several blankets until she found a large item made of leather. Pulling it out of the chest, she displayed for all to see. "Surprise!"

Thorik was speechless, and his grief of not going on the trip immediately vanished. "It's a pack! My very own backpack for our hikes."

"Yes, dear. I know you've been wanting one of these for a while now to store all of your papers and ink for notes and maps. Hopefully I've made it big enough for you to get some exploring and hunting gear in there as well."

He quickly put it on; it hung low, covering the boy's backside and pressing against the back of his legs. "It's perfect!"

"Well, maybe not today, but you'll grow into it."

"I have enough room in it to store everything from all of my adventures in distant lands. I can start by storing my coffer of maps. And a map of the valley beyond Spirit Peak would be a nice addition to it."

Su'I reached out and rustled up Thorik's hair. "When your parents return, they will have Runestones you can store in that fine pack. But I must warn you, young Num, not all adventures are full of fun... such as the time I was attacked by a Blothrud." His voice changed slightly, giving an air of mystery to the story he was about to tell.

His words caught the boy's attention enough to once again distract him from the journey he wanted to undertake. "What's a Blothrud?"

"A Blothrud is a mountain of a beast nearly twice your father's height, with a massive chest easily fourfold my very own. His legs are that of a wolf, and spikes poke out of his back and arms. But the worst part is his head. It has the snout of a dragon mixed with a hairless wolf. Hideous in nature and with a temper to boot. These creatures are the most dangerous of all the species. I had the unfortunate luck to run across one who wanted to see me dead."

Su'I continued with his stories of high adventure late into the evening. Thorik stared in amazement, when he wasn't studying the outsider's map. Thorik's father finished the tobacco in his pipe and stored it on a shelf near several books before helping his wife gather some blankets so the visitor could sleep on the floor. Since there was only one room in the home, it would be a full house for sleeping that night.

Chapter 4
Leaving

The next day started off warm and cloudy, much like many spring days in Farbank. It wasn't far into the day before Thorik and his mother arrived at Gluic's home, where Brimmelle opened the door to greet them.

Yawning and rubbing his eyes, Brimmelle opened the thick wooden door. "Hello?"

"Hello, brother," Thorik's mother was the only one that could put a smile on Brimmelle's sour face. "I need a favor from you."

"Absolutely. What can I do for you, my dear sister?"

"I need you to watch Thorik for a few nights while we take a short trip."

Thorik glanced in the home and caught a whiff of what he would term 'old people smell' from inside.

Brimmelle's face immediately changed back to his annoyed expression. "Why can't you take him with you?"

"Because I don't think it's safe for him."

"Then it is clearly not safe for you, either. Is your lazy husband making you go with him on some foolish slog? I could send him down to Longfield for a few years if you need some time away from him." As the spiritual leader of the village, he had the power to do so.

"Brimmelle, I'm asking you for a favor. Can you please do this for me?"

"The boy?" He glared down at him. "Is he house broken yet? I'm not going to clean up after him."

She gently placed her hands on his shoulders. "You won't even know he's here."

"Oh, I'll know."

"Dear brother, please do this for me."

Brimmelle gazed into his loving sister's eyes and nodded. "Only for you."

"I know."

Brimmelle changed his focus from her to her son. "But I'll be expecting him to help me with my teachings of the Words of Order."

Smiling, she replied, "I'm sure he'll enjoy that. He can be your Sec-in-training for a few days."

Thorik scrunched up his nose at the idea. "Can I go play at Old Man Sammal's oak tree?"

Brimmelle puffed up his chest and pushed his chin forward before looking down at his nephew. "No. We have chores to do and studies to recite."

Thorik straightened the oversized leather backpack and gave his mother a goodbye hug. "I'm old enough to go with you."

"I know, dear, but I'm just not ready for you to take such risks. I'll see you in a few days. Please be good."

Thorik glanced in the dark house once again and sighed. "I love you, Mum."

"I love you too, dear." And with that, she left the home and headed to the river to meet her husband and Su'I Sorat.

Thorik watched until she was out of sight before he turned and stepped into the home. The 'old person smell' filled his nose and caused him to sneeze.

"Are you sick? Is that why you're not going?"

"No, I'm not sick. Something just caught my nose wrong."

"Well, get used to it. You can set your pack down in the back room. Don't touch anything in there and don't bother unloading. You won't be staying long, and I don't want to be picking up or stepping on your toys."

"I don't have toys," Thorik mumbled.

"What's that? What did you say?"

"Yes, Uncle. No toys."

"You're old enough now that you should be referring to me as Fir Brimmelle like the rest of the village does."

"Yes, Uncle Fir."

"Don't get a spirited tongue around me, young man."

"Yes, Fir Brimmelle."

Hours went by as Brimmelle slowly and methodically followed his daily routine of preparing for the afternoon's teachings of the Mountain King's words.

Thorik was eventually able to pull out a single map to review without being in trouble for making a mess. It was a long, dull day until his grandmother, Gluic, arrived. "Granna!"

"Welcome, my dear. It's so good to see you." Colorful leaves and spring flowers garnished her clothes and hair, which she had collected during her morning walk and daily activities. Small pouches and purses, filled with small stones and various plant life, hung from her shoulders, neck, and arms. "You're here for a visit, I see."

"Yes, I will be staying with you for a few nights while my parents are on a trip to the far side of the river with our new friend, Su'I Sorat."

"Oh my. It's finally started. I didn't realize it would begin so soon. Although, I could feel the change in the rocks by the river this morning." As with all adult Nums, Gluic had darker patches of skin called soul-markings covering her body. Hers were fanciful and playful lines that changed to a darker shade upon hearing Thorik's news.

"What's started? What change?"

"Brimmelle! Start cleaning out the back room."

"Mother, the boy can sleep on the floor in the entryway. He will only be here for a few days."

"Yes, that's what Thorik said. Now, make my grandson comfortable."

"But mother, I have to prepare for my teachings this afternoon!"

"It's the same boring teachings you do every week. Give it a rest this once. I don't think it will cause everyone to run around in chaos from the lack of hearing your dry voice."

"Mother! I have a duty to perform. I don't think you take what I do seriously."

"I know, dear. You'll get over it."

Flustered, Brimmelle stormed out of the home, slamming the door behind him.

"Granna, I think you may have pushed him too hard that time."

"No, not yet. I'll get him there sooner or later."

Thorik laughed. "Why do you do that to him?"

"Because he has so much potential to help others with his knowledge, yet instead he lets his arrogance get in the way of truly reaching the people he's trying to help. Don't worry, dear. He has a long journey ahead of him, and today is the commencement of it."

"Is he going someplace?"

"Yes, dear. In fact, you are too. We all are." With that, Gluic went into the back room and started tossing Brimmelle's childhood items out the door into the main room of the house. "He kept a jar of his fingernail clippings? That boy has issues."

Gluic continued to toss out all of her son's memories in order to make way for a clean room to be used by Thorik. Despite her age, she was able to keep Thorik hopping, as the boy moved the items from the doorway to a pile just outside the front door.

This went on into the evening. It began to rain, and thunder could be heard in the distance. Brimmelle made his way home before a downpour began. Once he arrived, he was appalled at the stack of his items near the front door. "Mother!"

The sound of the lock could be heard from the inside of the door. "Yes, dear?" Gluic's voice was pleasant and uplifting.

Attempting to open the door, he confirmed he had just been locked out. "Open this door, mother!"

"Not with that tone in your voice, dear."

"You have got to be kidding me! It's raining out here!"

"Yes, it is. And I think it will get worse soon."

"Then let me in! I'm getting soaked, and all my treasures are being destroyed before my very eyes!"

"It's time to put your past behind you."

Lightning flashed and a loud rumbling of thunder rolled across the village.

"By destroying them?"

"No, dear. Your memories are not in those objects. They are in your heart and head. Those things before you are not important. They are just things. It's time for you to start caring more about the Nums in this village instead of hoarding objects."

Another flash snapped across the sky and was followed almost immediately by a crack of thunder that caused Brimmelle to jump flat against the door. "Why are you doing this right now?"

"Because it's time. And the fact that it's very dangerous out there makes you more open to being persuaded."

Lightning ripped overhead; this time close enough to make the hair on Brimmelle's arm to stand on end from the static charge. "Mother! You win! Let me in!"

The sound of the door being unlocked behind him was too soft compared to the heavy rain and thunder. The door flung open, causing him to fall backward into the home, slapping his wet body onto the floor.

"Don't just lay there, dear," Gluic mused. "Close the door before we catch ourselves a cold."

Brimmelle reached over with one leg and pushed the door closed.

"Thank you, dear. Welcome home. How was your day?"

Panting from fear of being struck by lightning, he continued to lie on the floor. "Same as usual."

"As expected." She set three bowls of soup at the table before sitting down next to where Thorik had been quietly watching the events unfold. "Supper is ready. Get some dry clothes on before joining us."

"Yes, mother." He then slowly rolled to one side and stood up before heading to his bedroom.

Thorik took several slow sips of soup before addressing her. "Granna, it's raining very hard out there."

"Yes, dear. It is."

"My parents are out in this. I hope they will be safe."

"I know, dear. It's natural to be concerned for their safety, just like they are concerned about yours."

Brimmelle returned in a robe while still drying his hair with a towel. Unlike his mother's whimsical soul-markings, his were broad strokes of darker skin that flowed from his left hand up to his strong jaw. His dark shades of hair surrounded his round face as well as his thick bushy eyebrows. "Where are your parents going anyway?"

Thorik swallowed his spoonful of soup before answering. "They are helping Su'l Sorat find a lost treasure."

"Su'l Sorat? He's the outsider who came to town yesterday, isn't he?"

"Yes."

"He's dangerous! I told him to leave us and never return. There would be nothing here for him in Farbank."

"Apparently he did as you asked and headed upstream of Farbank before finding us."

"This is not good. What did he want?"

"They are in search of the Mountain King's Runestones."

"What? They don't exist anymore. I've read the historical records. They were destroyed long ago. He must be leading them into a trap. I knew I should have told her that I wouldn't watch you. Then she would have been forced to stay."

"Then my father would have gone with him alone. He'd still be in danger."

"Yes, but that would be his fault for listening to an outsider."

"If my parents are in trouble, we need to save them!" Wanting to begin the search right away, Thorik jumped up from the table.

"Or at least my sister." Brimmelle began grabbing gear for a trek as they talked. "Where were they headed?"

"It's unclear. It was kind of a riddle of instructions."

"They had to know where they were going to start!"

"Yes! They headed across to the far side of the King's River and then past Spirit Peak. They were hoping to find a ghost who would point the way and then follow the grazer's path to some giant mouth."

With arms filled with gear, they both reached the front door just as a loud snap of thunder shook the entire home.

Still sitting at the table enjoying her soup, Gluic looked up at the two. "I'd wait until the morning." She then took another sip.

The heavy rain slammed against the roof and walls and worked its way in under the door. The storm was getting worse.

They both looked at each other and nodded. "Agreed."

Chapter 5
Stormy Nightmare

The storm was relentless as the night went on. Winds blew hard and rain struck the earth with an intensity that few storms reach. The lightning and thunder eventually faded off but never completely left the river valley. In spite of the noise, everyone eventually fell asleep.

Sleep led to dreams and dreams led to visions of his parents struggling in the storm. Jolting awake, Thorik woke up from a nightmare and raced into his grandmother's room. Her eyes were open, but she was clearly sound asleep. "Granna! They're in danger! We need to leave to save them."

"What's going on?" Brimmelle yelled from his room.

Thorik turned and raced to his uncle's bedroom. "I know this sounds crazy, but I had this dream that my parents are in great danger. I need to save them!"

"Of course we will. We'll leave once the storm subsides."

"It's calmed down to a drizzle. We can leave now."

"Thorik Dain, my sister left you in my control, and I am not allowing you to race off in the middle of a stormy night because you had a dream. So get back to bed before I tie you to the bedposts!"

Thorik wiped the tears from his face and ran back to his room. He could only hope that he was wrong. Unfortunately, he couldn't stop thinking about it. It seemed so real.

After a few hours of tormenting himself for not doing anything to help them, Thorik gathered his items, along with some of his grandmother's baked goods, and put them in his backpack before sneaking out of the house and to the river.

Low laying, dark clouds limited his vision until the storm began to move out of the river valley. He took this as good sign as he jumped into a rowboat and made his way across to the far shoreline.

Knowing Spirit Peak's location was simple after all the time he had taken reviewing the maps. The challenge would be finding it at night. Distant lighting assisted him as he made his way on foot through the open forest, toward the Eldoric Mountain Range.

By the time he reached the point he was looking for, morning light was starting to shine upon Spirit Peak. Again, this appeared to be a good omen since the sun pierced through the clouds and brightened the peak for him to view. He was feeling fortunate despite walking all night.

Closing in on the tall column of rock known as Spirit Peak, he began to grow concerned. He had never traveled beyond this point and needed to determine which way to proceed. The hillsides were steep and the ground was loose. It was obvious why his parents didn't want him to climb these mountain foothills. "The ghost will point the way," he said to himself. Glancing about, he continued to hike past the peak. Frustrated at having no path to follow, he eventually glanced back at the peak and noticed that he was now in the shadow of the rock column. "Perhaps the shadow of Spirit Peak is pointing the way." He had no better plan, so he went with it.

Moving as quickly as he could on the wet mountain terrain, he started to struggle again. "How do I go in the direction of the peak's shadow if the sun keeps moving?" Continuing to modify his search, it wasn't long before the peak was going in a completely different direction than he was originally heading. "This is insane! I have no idea which way to go!" To add insult to injury, the rain started up again.

With a lack of options, the young Num headed uphill in order to get a better view of his surroundings. It was during this climb that he slipped and began to slide down the mountainside. Tumbling and rolling on rocks, muddy ledges, and bushes, he finally came to a stop.

Looking up, he was inches away from an animal carcass. The smell was awful, and the animal's skin had been stripped off; its head was hanging limp to one side. It was a dead Grazer.

Initially, the sight struck fear in the youth, but his emotions quickly turned to excitement. Gathering his footing, he searched about for a potential second carcass, and to his luck he found the old bones of another Grazer several yards away from him.

Heading past the second body, he again searched for another. His assumption was correct. "The Grazer's path that we are looking for is not the actual path they leave. It's is a path of dead Grazers."

He continued to follow the trail of bones and flesh for most of the day. The path eventually ended at a cave entrance which, from the correct angle, appeared like the mouth of a giant face. "This must be it."

With the storm increasing again, the idea of getting in a cave seemed very welcoming. At least it did until he was a few dozen yards into it and began smelling dead flesh. Perhaps it was more Grazers. "What's been killing these Grazers?" he muttered to himself after realizing that his single focus of finding his parents had prevented him from seeing the obvious. "There is a creature here that is killing these animals and most likely lives in this cave."

His heart raced as he stopped mid stride and listened to the noises within the cave. All seemed quiet. Then, with a glance back at the front entrance to the cave, Thorik could see several eyes trained on his position as a pack of grey wolves prepared to attack.

Thorik bolted deeper into the cave, hoping to find something to save himself from being eaten alive.

The wolves gave chase after the Num. It wouldn't take long for them to catch up.

Hearing the wolves snapping at his heels, Thorik made a leap up one side of the cavern to a small ledge. Grabbing it with both hands, he swung his legs up onto the rock shelf before rolling the rest of his body onto it.

The wolves repeatedly attempted to run up the side of the wall in fruitless attempts to reach him. He was safe, yet he was trapped. It would be a long night for the young Num as he waited out the wolves.

Chapter 6
The Valley Beyond

Waking up to the sounds of a bird poking at his pack to get at the food he had tucked away before leaving his grandmother's home, Thorik realized it was time to get moving again. The wolves were gone, but he didn't know which way they had traveled. He had followed the instructions and found the Old Man's Mouth, but he still hadn't found the Runestones or his parents. If Su'l Sorat's directions were correct, the cave should lead him to the valley where the treasure was hidden.

Sitting up on the ledge, Thorik watched a bird fly past him, deeper into the cavern. "If you can get out that way, hopefully I can as well."

Ever so quietly, he lowered himself back to the cavern floor and headed away from the entrance. The light slowly dissipated, and just as it did, a new light source began to fill the cave in front of him. There definitely was a second entrance, and this one led to a new valley.

He quickly realized that he had overslept; it was already midday. If his parents were on the far side of the valley, he would be lucky to reach them before dark. "Where are you?" he asked.

Stepping out of the cavern and out to the end of an outcropping, he gazed at the green valley below and the muddy and rocky terrain along the upper valley walls. Several small rivers had carved wide paths when filled by heavy snow melts and led to a grassy open end of the valley. Squinting, he searched for his parents with broad gazing strokes across the entire region. "They have to be here someplace."

Patience was key, as he decided to comb through the valley with his eyes. In order to focus on one small area at a time, he made long, slow gazing passes. It finally paid off when he spotted figures moving on the far side, just above the tree line. It was now just a race against time.

Light on his feet, Thorik raced down the hillside, avoiding trees and rocks along the way. One wrong leap and he could break a leg or even fall to his death. He felt that he had to take the risk before his parents moved too far from where he had spotted them.

The lower valley was the most stressful. Thorik was able to move quickly, but the trees had obstructed his view; he could only guess as to his parent's location.

Leaping from boulder to fallen tree, over streams and crevasses, Thorik gave everything he could to race up the far valley hillside. He actually reached the tree line on the opposite side sooner than he had anticipated. Once there, he struggled to breathe as he spun around looking for his parents.

In the time it had taken him to cross the valley, another isolated storm had rolled in. Dark clouds were blown in over the mountain range. The rains immediately returned in an unexpected deluge. The ground was so saturated that any new precipitation ran freely down the sides of the valley. Sheets of rain poured down so violently that waves of water collected momentum throughout the valley.

Trees began to uproot and loose rock outcroppings gave way. The land itself was now too dangerous to be on, and there was nowhere to be surefooted.

The ground began to shift under his feet, and Thorik could feel the vibration of each tremor below him. The challenge, however, was from above him as a mudslide rolled down the valley's walls toward him.

His instincts kicked in, and before he even realized what he was doing he was in a race for his life back down the hill, and through the trees, toward the nearest stream. The sounds of timber snapping and falling behind him added adrenaline, but his muscles had been taxed to their limits, and he couldn't move any faster.

Reaching the stream's wide wash area, Thorik jumped back over the stones he had used when crossing the first time. As he leaped from the final stone the mudslide slapped against the ledge, bordering the wash basin of the stream, and sprayed the youth with muddy water before turning and flowing down the open wash area.

The heavy winds continued to blow the thundercloud up the opposite foothill, over the crest, and into the next valley. As quick as it had arrived, the heavy storm had passed, leaving only a soft misty rain behind. Random lightning persisted high in the clouds, but the damage in the valley had been done.

Trees and boulders continued to tumble into the stream, along with what appeared to be his mother's cloak clinging to a large limb. It wasn't long before the thick mud eventually slowed to a crawl along the expansion of the stream's sides. Minor landslides lost momentum, leaving the flowing water to carve a path down the middle of the mud-caked area.

Thick as paste, the once small stream in a large river wash was now a wide, slow-moving, muddy mess filled with everything the rain had uprooted from the hillsides.

"Mum?" Thorik jogged along the far side of the bank to keep up with her cloak, hoping to find her nearby. He soon found some additional hiking gear floating on the surface and other items he recognized stuck in trees, but his parents were not to be seen. "Mum! Father! Are you there?"

He continued to yell until he heard a distant cry for help. Listening closely, he traced it to an area filled thick with branches. Assuming it was his mother, he jumped into the dense, muddy streambed and pulled himself over to where he had heard the noise. Once there, he removed several limbs before finding her, just as she fell unconscious. "Mum! Wake up! It's me, Thorik!"

With the light rain working against him, he yanked more limbs and debris away in a nearly futile effort to pull her body free. "Mum! You have to help! I can't do this on my own."

Slowly opening her eyes, she immediately knew she was trapped as the slow rolling mud was sucking them both under. "Save yourself, Thorik," she said while pushing against a heavy branch to keep her head above the surface. "I made a mistake. I should have been more cautious, like my brother. I'm sorry."

Lightning snapped across the valley and thunder echoed against the stone walls as additional rain softened the muddy river, causing it to start moving quicker again. Trees underneath the surface locked against boulders and launched themselves up into the air. Limbs began to fling back and forth as though they had come alive while others became lodged into place and created dams for floating debris.

The softening of the mud did allow Thorik to pull his mother up and onto an old rotted tree trunk. He held onto her with one hand while clinging to the tree with the other.

The flowing mud pulled at their bodies as he struggled to retain his grip on the mud covered bark. His fingers burned as he held on for not only his life, but also that of his mothers.

A crash of lighting and thunder occurred at the same time, setting a nearby tree on fire. Rain increased, and the river began to flow faster. The fluid movement pulled them from the tree trunk as well as from each other. They were being washed away.

Everything seemed to be working against Thorik until he felt a sudden push back upstream, toward the tree, by his mother. She had been given him the gift of the momentary support of a newly lodged branch under the surface. But it came at a price; her hand slipped away from her son's. "I will always love you," she shouted before being swallowed by the muddy river.

Thorik screamed in horror as the rain pounded upon his body. Clutching the tree, he tried to wish it all away as though it was a bad dream. The vision of her washing away would be ingrained in his mind to the end of his days. Then again, his own mortality could very well end within the next few minutes, as another branch slapped him in the face.

"Grab it!" yelled an unexpected voice.

Thorik looked around for the origin, hoping desperately that it was his father, only to find his Uncle Brimmelle standing along the shoreline holding a limb out for Thorik to grab.

"Hurry up!" Reaching out as far as he could, Fir Brimmelle prodded the boy in order to wake him from his own fear. "You're lucky Gluic told me you'd be here!"

Struggling to let even one finger soften its grip, his muscles stayed locked into position, even though his mind wanted to grab the branch to safety. "Save Mum! She's just downstream!"

"Thorik Dain, you do as I say! Grab this branch right now!"

Somehow the direct order from his uncle caused enough of its own fear that it released him from the terror of the mudslide. As one hand freed itself to grab the branch to safety, a loud thunderclap shook the valley and triggered an even larger mudslide as a massive layer of the valley wall dislodged and began roaring down toward them, collecting everything in its path.

Brimmelle stepped back from the ledge and fought his instinct to run for safety from the horrific sight. His internal struggle of fear inadvertently caused him to pull the branch away from his nephew.

Thorik's free hand reached out and missed the branch as it was pulled away from him. It was like some bad hoax to tease the boy, leaving him dangling in the waterway clinging by one hand as new branches and bushes and even rocks slapped up against him from the surging mud flow.

His uncle stood frozen with his own fear as lightning raced overhead in a spectacular display of power. His eyes darted from the mountainside barreling down at them to Thorik and then downstream.

"Uncle Brimmelle!" Thorik screamed as loud as he could to catch the Num's attention. "Fir Brimmelle!"

Snapping out of it, his uncle braced himself the best he could along the ledge and reached forward with the branch.

Thorik fought against the stream's current to turn his body enough to reach out once again for the branch. He was exhausted, and this would be his last attempt. It was then that the decayed tree he had been holding onto snapped into pieces from the flood's pressure.

Pushing past the point of safety, Brimmelle leaned out further just in time to allow Thorik's free hand to grab the branch.

Being dragged by the mudslide's flow, Thorik hung on as Brimmelle attempted to stay in place, allowing the end of the branch to make an arc to the shore downstream. Once there, Thorik quickly grabbed at the ledge of the wash and pulled himself to safety.

However, safety was only temporary. The larger mudslide was nearly on top of them, and it would easily blow over the top of the existing river wash and onto the other side where they now stood. Massive trees snapped from their roots as the twenty foot wave of debris slammed through the forest, devouring all in its path.

Grabbing Thorik by the shirt, Brimmelle began to race up the opposite hill to avoid certain death. The ground was slick, and they weren't more than a few steps into the woods when he slipped, tossing Thorik forward to the ground. His eyes darted back to the mudslide, and once again he fell into a trance-like state. He had never felt such terror.

Thorik returned and shook his uncle out of his daze. "Uncle! We have to keep running!" Helping his uncle to his feet, the two moved up the far hillside as quickly as their bodies would allow.

The valley continued to rumble as the massive wall of rocks and mud consumed the landscape. Rolling into and over the stream, it sloshed its way across to the other side and sloshed several dozen yards up onto the opposite hill. Fortunately the river depleted enough of the energy to prevent it catching up to the Nums, who had fallen to their knees, out of breath and strength.

Exhausted, Thorik and Brimmelle watched the events unfold from their new vantage point up the hill. It somehow didn't seem true, yet it was all too real to handle. Mesmerized by the sight, they sat there and watched as the rain eventually moved on, the sun made an appearance, and the mud thickened and stopped flowing.

Downstream a bit, the mud had washed out onto open, flat grasslands, causing the boulders and trees to stick out of the now thin layer of drying mud. It was a wide swath of land coated with debris from everything the mudslide had swallowed in its path.

"We have to find my parents," Thorik said softly to his uncle, who wasn't in a frame of mind to argue about anything.

It was an undertaking that lasted an entire day before they found his parent's bodies. Su'I Sorat, however, was never unearthed. Few comments were spoken by Thorik, while his uncle never uttered a word. Grief and anger had consumed the elder Num.

Thorik stood alone, even when Brimmelle was near. He had lost his family; the ones he loved. He was also stricken with guilt; he believed the loss of his parents had been entirely his fault. He was angry, ashamed, and distraught. With so many emotions tugging at him, he didn't know what to do, other than keep busy.

Brimmelle helped Thorik pull the bodies out of the muddy open area. His parents would be placed side by side in a single large grave for the two of them to spend the afterlife together, holding hands for eternity. After straightening their clothes, and wiping their faces clean of mud, Thorik took a few moments with each of his parents as Brimmelle struggled to make eye contact with him.

Wrapped around the body of Thorik's father was a satchel that contained an ancient, beaten-up, sealed metal box. Upon searching inside it, Thorik found a sack with a note on it which read, 'Happiest of birthday wishes, my son. You are special, just like these stones.' It was a card that his father had filled out before leaving on his journey in the hope that he could finally give his son a unique birthday gift. A slight tearful smile crossed Thorik's face as he recalled how often his parents told him how special he was. Opening the sack, he found several dozen flat hexagonal Runestones with gems embedded into them.

"They found the treasure and were on their way back." Thorik stared at the note in his father's handwriting. "Thank you, father. You always said that one of these days you would give me something unique. However, I would have never asked for it if I knew the high cost."

Turning toward his mother, his lips thinned and began to tremble. "You sacrificed yourself to save me, Mum. I'm sorry I wasn't here soon enough. I tried, but I failed. I hope you'll forgive me." Placing his hand into hers, he rocked back and forth for a bit. "I wish we could dance again. I should have spent more time with you when I had the opportunity. What I wouldn't give for just one more moment to tell you that I love you, Mum." Breaking down, he collapsed onto his mother and cried until his stomach and chest muscles hurt too much to continue. He had nothing else to give. He was depleted.

The long silence was eventually broken as Thorik wiped his eyes and said to Brimmelle, "It's time to move them into their final resting place." Once his parents were in the wide, shallow grave, the young Num had his final words with them. "I didn't realize how fortunate I was to have you until it was too late. I took your love for granted. I assumed you would always be around to bring a smile on my face when I felt sad or encourage me to try again when I had failed at a task. Your efforts to teach me morals through your actions instead of your words were overlooked until today. But I pledge this to you, my parents; I will not let you down again. I will never take for granted the opportunity I get with anyone that comes into my life. I will do the right thing, whenever possible, and as often as possible. I will make you proud of me, I promise this to you both."

Brimmelle kept his eyes from the boy's view as tears ran down his face.

"Thank you," Thorik continued. "Thank you for giving me what you had. Not wealth or power, but love, trust, and respect. You have given me more than any son could ever ask for." Wiping his own tears once again, he straightened up and pulled his shoulders back. "May you find each other in the afterlife."

Chapter 7
Home

Days later, back in Farbank, Gluic tucked Thorik and Brimmelle into their beds to rest their weary bodies from their travels and hardships. Each received a sympathetic hand to their foreheads before she left their individual rooms.

Returning to the main room of her home, she picked up Thorik's leather backpack and set it on her table. The stitching was just as she had taught her daughter to do in order to ensure it would last for ages.

Opening the pack, she reached in and pulled out the sack of Runestones before untying the string on top, opening it wide, and viewing the stones inside. The flat hexagonal stones had colored crystals in the center, while most had various colored gems at the corners. Arching stone ridges filled the surface areas in their own unique patterns. Each was a symbol with its own meaning.

Reaching into the sack, she sighed with relief. "These are good stones. Full of energy, and stories, and life." A smile grew on her face as the center crystal of each and every Runestone began to glow, filling the room with beams of light. A sense of calmness filled her body.

Moving one hand deeper within the sack, she searched for a specific Runestone toward the bottom. Once found, Gluic pulled it from the rest, causing the room to go dark except for the light emanating from the crystal in the stone she held before her.

This specific Runestone had a center crystal unlike the rest. Instead of a single color, the crystal gave off a range of colors from within it. The various shades and hues pulsed brighter at the ever-changing frequencies as the elder Num gazed into its light. Dimming, a single swirl of light could be seen deep inside the crystal. "Ah, there you are, my daughter. Welcome home." The crystal grew more intense, and the room filled with light once again. "Yes, dear. I will look after your son. He has an amazing adventure before him that will make you proud."

www.AlteredCreatures.com

Altered Creatures Epic Adventures continues with the following:

Nums of Shoreview Series (Pre-Teen, Ages 9 to 12)
Stolen Orb (Book 1)
Unfair Trade (Book 2)
Slave Trade (Book 3)
Baka's Curse (Book 4)
Haunted Secrets (Book 5)
Rodent Buttes (Book 6)

Thorik Dain Series (Young Adult and Adult)
Treasure of Sorat (Prequel)
Fate of Thorik (Book 1)
Sacrifice of Ericc (Book 2)
Essence of Gluic (Book 3)
Rise of Rummon (Book 4)
Prey of Ambrosius (Book 5)
Plea of Avanda (Book 6)

Tilli of Kingsfoot Series (Young Adult and Adult)
Time Will Tell

Santorray's Privations Series (Adult)
Hunted
Outraged

Look for other upcoming stories of
Santorray's Privations
Tilli of Kingsfoot
Darkmere
Myth'Unday
Dragon & Del'Unday Wars
and more...

CHARACTERS Pronunciation Guide
Brimmelle: brim-uhl
Dovenar: doh-ven-ahr
E'rudite: ee-roo-dahyt
Feshlan: fesh-luhn
Gluic: gloo-ik
Irluk: ur-luhk
Su'I Sorat: Soo-ee-sohr-at
Thorik: thawr-ik
Wyrlyn: wur-lin

LOCATIONS Pronunciation Guide
Farbank: far-bangk
Luthralum: loo-thrawl-uhm
Lu'Tythis: loo-tith-is
Woodlen: wood-len

SPECIES Pronunciation Guide

Blothrud (AKA Ruds): bloth-ruhd
7' to 9' tall; Bony hairless dragon-like head; Red muscular human torso and arms; Sharp spikes extend out across shoulder blades, back of arms, and back of hands; Red hair covered waist and over two thick strong wolf legs. Blothruds are typically the highest class of the Del'Undays.

Brandercat: brand-er-kat
Large lion-sized cats that have scales instead of hair. They can change the color of their scales to turn nearly invisible.

Del'Unday: del-oon-dey
The Del'Unday are a collection of Altered Creatures who live in structured communities with rules and strong leadership. These include Blothruds, Wolvians, Brandercats.

E'rudite: EE-roo-dIt
The E'rudite aren't actually a species. They are typically humans that have been trained in the basic arts of the Notarian mind control powers which makes them much more powerful than others, but not nearly that of a Notarian.

Fesh'Unday: fesh-oon-dey

The Fesh'Unday are all of the Altered Creatures that roam freely without societies. Wolves, boars, raccoons, and most forest creatures are in this clan.

Gathler: gath-ler

6' to 8' tall; Giant sloth-like species; Gathlers are the leaders of the Ov'Undays. They are very curious creatures who take their time to investigate the true nature of things.

Human: hyoo-muhn

5' to 6' tall; pale to dark complexion; weight varies from anorexic to obese. Most live within the Dovenar Kingdom.

Krupes: kroop

6' to 8' tall; Covered from head to toe in black armor, these thick and heavy bipedal creatures move slow but are difficult to defeat. Few have seen what they look like under their armor. Krupes are the soldiers of the Del'Unday.

Mognin (AKA Mogs): mawg-nin

10' to 12' tall; Mognins are the tallest of the Ov'Unday.

Myth'Unday: mith-oon-dey

The Myth'Unday are a collection of Creatures brought to life by altering nature's plants and insects.

Notarian: noh-tawr-ee-in

These thin human-like creatures have semi-translucent skin and no natural hair anywhere on their bodies. Their motions are smooth and graceful and they have incredible mental powers that appear to be god-like to the other species.

Ov'Unday: ov-oon-dey

The Ov'Unday are a collection of Altered Creatures who believe in living as equals in peaceful communities. Typically pacifists. Species such as Mognins and Gathers are part of this clan.

Polenum (AKA Nums): pol-uh-nuhm

4' to 5' tall; Human-like features; Very pale skin; Soul-markings cover their bodies in thin or thick lines as they mature. Exceptional eyesight.